JUST CAI

MERCER MAYER

A GOLDEN BOOK • NEW YORK
Western Publishing Company, Inc., Racine, Wisconsin 53404

We went camping in the backyard,
just my brother and me.

We hung our lantern.

We unrolled our sleeping bags.

We pitched our tent.

Dad was nearby, so he helped a little.

It was beginning to get dark.
We ate the sandwiches that Mom had made.

But we were still hungry, so...

we went inside. Weren't we lucky!
Mom had made spaghetti.
We had some of that, too.

Then Mom filled our canteens full of lemonade,
and we went back outside.

But we weren't sleepy,
and there wasn't too much to do...

so we went inside for a while to watch TV.

There was nothing really good on TV, but we started giggling anyway.
Dad said, "The campers should either go camping or upstairs to bed."

We asked Dad to walk us back to our tent,
not because we were scared...

but because we wanted
him to read us a story.

We turned off the lantern.
Dad went back inside.
It was dark.

Really dark.

Something jumped on our tent.
"What was that?" I asked.

It was just my kitty.

"I think my teddy bear misses me.
And the ground is too lumpy," I said.

Camping out is really fun for playing.
But it's not too good for sleeping...

so I went inside.

I'll go camping again tomorrow.